Siddhartha
and the Swan

Andrew Fusek Peters
Illustrated by Miss Swanne

A & C Black • London

White Wolves series consultant: Sue Ellis,
Centre for Literacy in Primary Education

This book can be used in the White Wolves Guided Reading
programme by readers who need a lot of support in Year 2

First published 2012 by
A & C Black
Bloomsbury Publishing Plc
50 Bedford Square
London
WC1B 3DP

www.acblack.com

Text copyright © 2012 Andrew Fusek Peters
Illustrations copyright © 2012 Miss Swanne/Folioart.co.uk

ISBN 978-1-4081-3947-9

A CIP catalogue for this book is available from the British Library.

This book is produced using paper that is made from wood
grown in managed, sustainable forests. It is natural, renewable
and recyclable. The logging and manufacturing processes conform
to the environmental regulations of the country of origin.

Printed and bound in China by C&C Offset Printing Co.

Chapter 1

It was a warm spring evening. Prince
Siddhartha was walking by the lake near
the palace when he heard a strange,
swooshing sound.

The prince looked up into the sky. He
saw three white swans flying high overhead.
The sight filled his heart with joy.

4

Suddenly, one of the swans gave a terrible screech. The wings of the swan stopped beating.

The poor bird fell down towards the ground. Someone had shot the swan!

Chapter 2

The prince ran to find the fallen bird.

It lay on the grass, crying in great pain. An arrow was sticking out of its shoulder.

"Who could have shot such a beautiful bird?" he cried. He felt sad. What could he do?

Prince Siddhartha knelt down and began to stroke its soft feathers.

"I too was a swan in a past life!" he said to the bird.

"Do not be afraid. I only wish to help."
Soon, the swan began to calm down.

The prince leaned over and gently pulled the arrow out. Then he wrapped his shirt round the swan to keep it warm.

13

Chapter 3

Someone shouted loudly. "Where is it?"

It was Devadatta, cousin of the prince.
He carried a large bow.

"Well done, cousin. You've found my swan!"

"It's not your swan," the prince replied.
"It's wild and belongs only to the sky!"

"But I shot it!" his cousin said. "So it's mine. That's the law."

"It might be the law. But this swan is still alive. I wish to help her get better."

His cousin was furious. "I've never heard anything so stupid!"

"Well," said Siddhartha quietly, "why don't we go to see the king and his wise ministers? They can help us settle the argument."

Chapter 4

There was a big debate in the court.

Devadatta said, "If I shoot an animal, the law says it belongs to me."

The ministers agreed.

Siddhartha made his point. "Only if
the bird is dead! This swan is still alive."
Now, nobody knew what to do.

Suddenly, an old man appeared in the
doorway.

"What if the swan could speak?" he said. "The swan would say that she wanted to get well again. Nobody wishes to feel pain or die. The swan should go to whoever wants to give it life."

The king spoke up. "Wise words
indeed. But let both boys look after the
swan!"

Chapter 5

Devadatta finally realised that animals felt pain too. He agreed to help Siddhartha care for the swan. Soon, it was well again.

One night, they were walking down by the lake near the palace when they heard a strange, swooshing sound.

"Look!" said Devadatta. He pointed up at the sky. "The other swans have come back for her!"

The healed swan tried beating her wings.

Slowly, slowly, she rose up into the air and climbed into the dusk.

Siddhartha and his cousin watched as the swans flew off towards the mountains.

Years later, the prince grew up to become the Buddha. He taught people to be kind to all living creatures.